"...and the Big Bad Wolf stamped
his feet all the way home."

We all have a Big Bad Wolf loping around inside of us.
A wild beast who likes to snap and growl sometimes.
And there's nothing we can do about it.

Or is there?

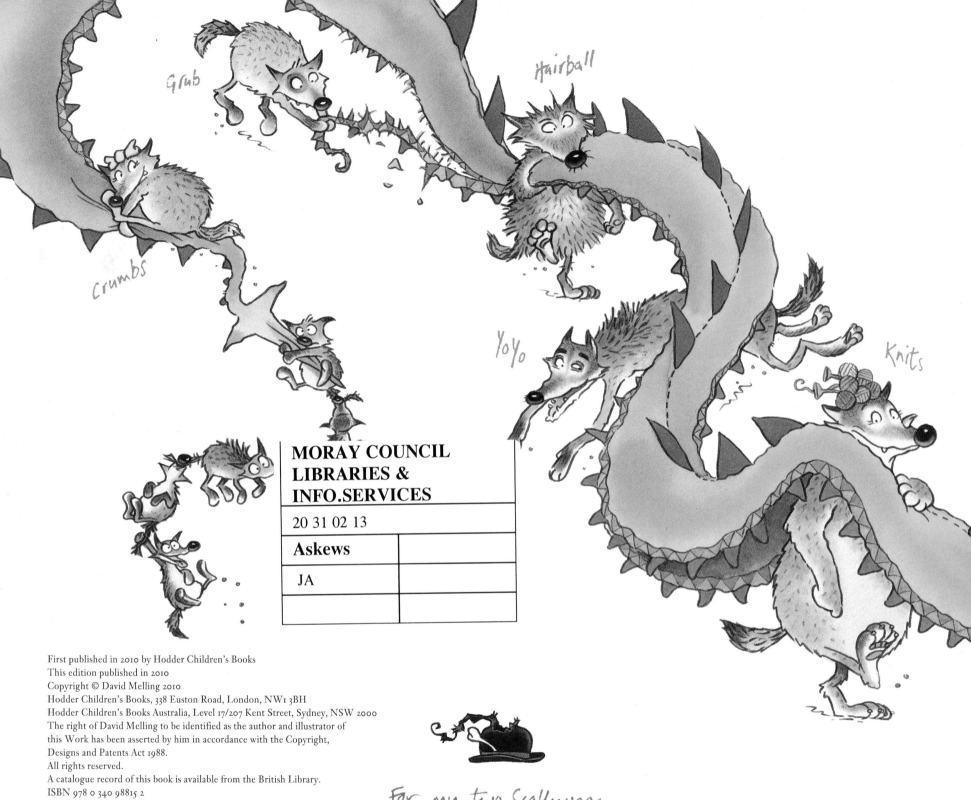

Grub

Hairball

crumbs

YoYo

Knits

First published in 2010 by Hodder Children's Books

This edition published in 2010

Copyright © David Melling 2010

Hodder Children's Books, 338 Euston Road, London, NW1 3BH

Hodder Children's Books Australia, Level 17/207 Kent Street, Sydney, NSW 2000

The right of David Melling to be identified as the author and illustrator of
this Work has been asserted by him in accordance with the Copyright,
Designs and Patents Act 1988.

All rights reserved.

A catalogue record of this book is available from the British Library.

ISBN 978 0 340 98815 2

10 9 8 7 6 5 4 3 2 1

Printed in China

Hodder Children's Books is a division of Hachette Children's Books,
an Hachette UK Company

www.hachette.co.uk

For my two scallywags
Monika and Luka

A division of Hachette Children's Books

Hodder
Children's
Books

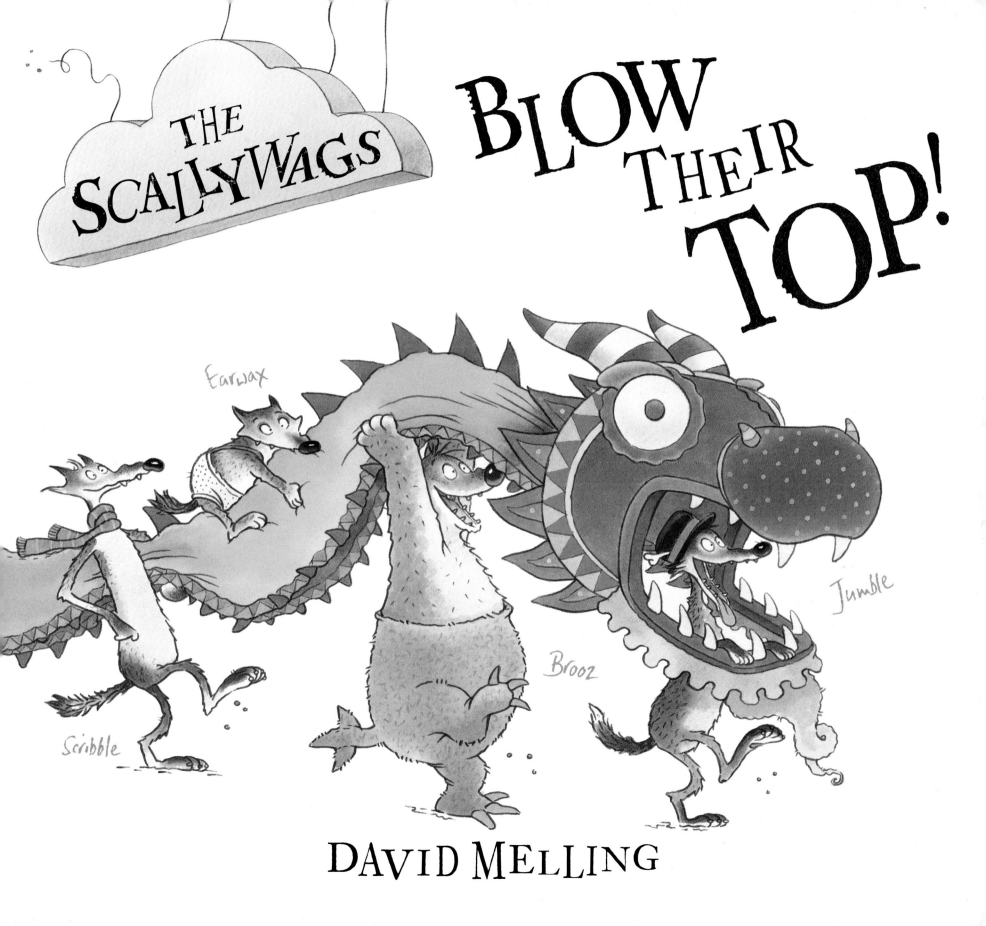

This story begins one bright crisp morning when all the animals were getting ready to put on a show. It was a fairy tale story and everyone was very excited.

But there was a problem.

Trouble was bubbling inside the dragon.

The wolves were losing their tempers.

'Stop pushing,' complained Knits.

'I can't help it, I'm sticking out the back,' growled Grub.
'Anyway, I don't want to be the tail. Why can't I be the head –
it smells down this end!'

'Don't care,' said Jumble, 'I'm the leader,
so I'm the head!'
'That's not fair!' shouted Grub.

'Will you Scallywags stop
arguing!' cried the Queen.

Of course, it got worse.

There were **howls** of anger. Teeth flashed, bottoms were bitten. The dragon squirmed and bulged and…
Rip!
Out spilled the wolves.

'**Look what you've done,**' wailed the other animals. 'Go away, just go away, all of you!'

The Scallywags picked up the costume and s t a m p e d off in a huff.

The wolves grumbled and growled all the way back to their tree house.

'That was your fault for **pushing!**'

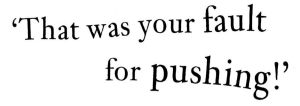

'Your fault for **smelling!**'

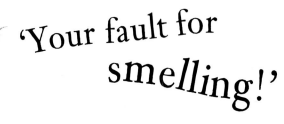

'Your fault for **biting!**'

Then they all pointed at Grub. 'It was **your** fault for having that temper!'

Grub wasn't listening.
He'd spotted something
by the tree house.

It was a little sheep.

The Scallywags forgot about being cross and trotted over to take a closer look. They gathered round and gave this new thing a good long sniff all over.

The little sheep frowned. She didn't like being close to so many noses so she plucked a hair from the biggest one.

'Ow!' said Brooz, 'That dun-half hurt!'

'Let's play!' said the little sheep sweetly. 'I'll be the princess and you can be the dragon!'

The wolves wagged their tails. They loved playing games. 'Who cares about that mouldy old show?' they sniggered.

'First off,' said the little sheep loudly, 'I'm the Pink Princess, so one of you has to put me in the tree house. That'll be my tower.'

She made them line up, then prodded Grub. 'You can carry me!

Then, when I'm ready I'll tell you what to do!'

'She's a bit bossy,' whispered Grub. But the little sheep heard him.

When the princess was in her tower she looked down and sniffed.
'**Right, listen up everyone,**' said the little sheep.
'This is the game. You have to climb up and
catch me and I have to try and stop you.'
'Easy!' said the wolves.

But it wasn't.

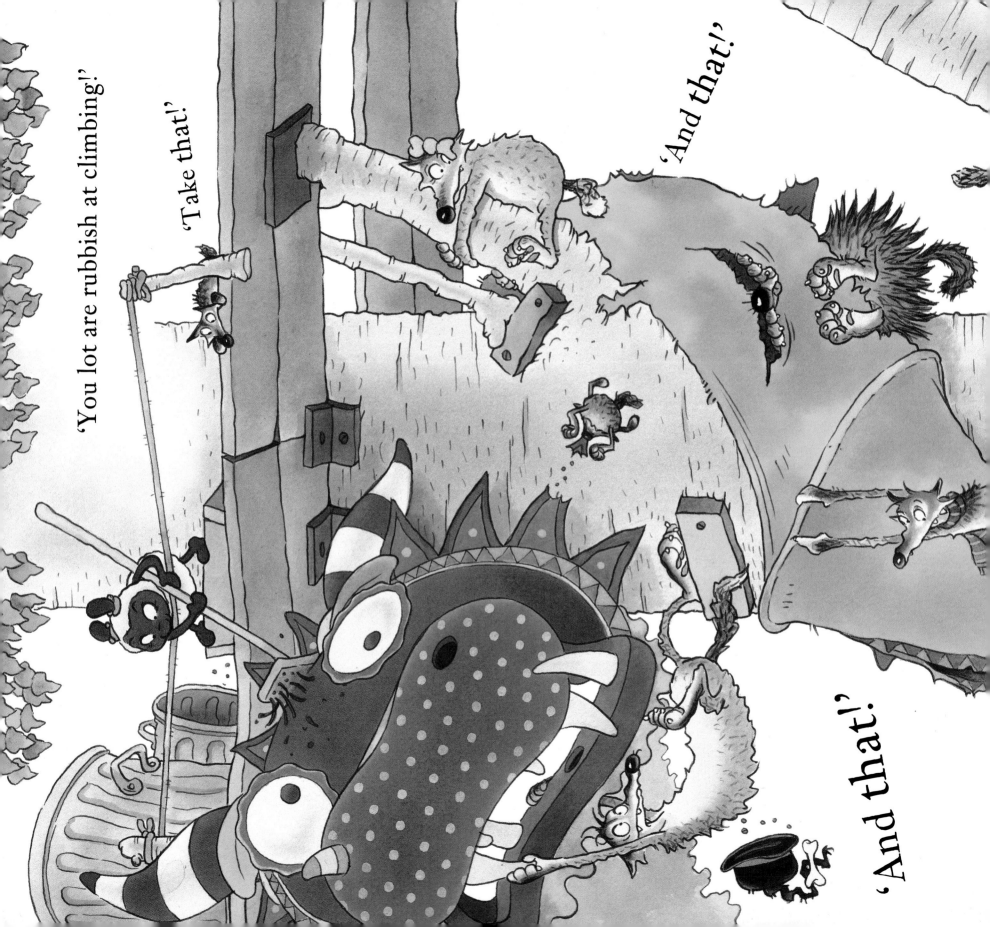

Finally, the wolves had had enough.

'Why don't you climb up if you're so clever!' snapped Yoyo.

'Because I'm the Pink Princess, you dozy doughnut!' squealed the little sheep.

'Oooh!' said the Scallywags. 'Temper, temper!' But one look at the little sheep and the wolves wished they hadn't said that.

The little princess wobbled.
She screwed up her face and…

'WHAAAAAAAH!'

The dragon finally let go of the tree and crumpled
to the floor.

Jumble was the first to escape. 'Quick,' he said.
'Leg it!'
'NO!' cried the little sheep. 'Come back.
We haven't finished the game!'

The Scallywags raced back
to the other animals and asked
them for a second chance.

'Will you promise not to get cross,
and argue and shout?' said the Queen.

The wolves looked at each other. They thought about the game
with the little sheep and nodded. 'Yes,' they said, 'we do!'

So that was how the Scallywags managed to join in nicely without losing their tempers. If they did get hot and bothered and wanted to bite someone,

they remembered how they felt when the little sheep was cross with **them**.
And the show finished happily ever after…

...until the little sheep found them and wanted to be the head of the

dragon.